**The Urbana Free Library**

To renew: call **217-367-4057**
or go to **urbanafreelibrary.org**
and select **My Account**

# the Masterpiece

Written by
## Shelley Kinder

Illustrated by
## Kathi Green Nixon

Summary:
God paints a sunrise onto a deep blue sky as families
get ready for school and admire the vibrant colors of
the Master Painter's creation.

Clear Fork Publishing
P.O. Box 870
102 S. Swenson
Stamford, Texas 79553
(325)773-5550
www.clearforkpublishing.com

Printed and Bound in the United States of America

ISBN - 9781946101655
LCN - 2018946979

www.clearforkpublishing.com

To God - Thank you for loving us like you do. I pray this book glorifies your name.

To Scott - Thank you for loving me and my writing mind.

To Shane, Aaron, Summer, and Micah - Always. Never cease to revel in the beauty around you.

To Mom - Thank you for raising me with a heart of love, humility, and vulnerability. And for putting everything you had into this book.

To the music makers of the world who help bring me into God's presence. I'm a better writer, and human, in that place.

Shelley

To Shelley - my favorite author, who also happens to be a pretty great daughter and friend. Thank you for this awesome opportunity!

To Kristy and Chad - for just being your amazing selves and teaching me so much along the way. I'm so proud of you both!

To Doug - for putting up with me day after day as I lived in my studio rarely to be seen. I'll make it up to you, Honey!

To Dad - for passing on your love and talent for art and all things creative.

To my awesome God - for creating such a beautiful world that inspires me every day and for loving me just the way I am.

Kathi

Deep blue canvas.
Passionate Painter.

"Let me color your morning,"
He says.

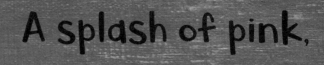

A splash of pink,

a streak of orange,

dashes of yellow.

A little boy shouts, "Pretty!"
The Painter smiles.

He adds **more** pink,

**more** yellow,
**MORE** orange,

and a **punch** of purple!

The Painter is pleased.

People point,

cheer,

dance!

"Could anything be more
beautiful?" they ask.

"**YOU**," says the Painter.

He rests his brush,
excited for sunset.

Oh, the possibilities!

1975

Kathi & Shelley

2018

Shelley & Kathi

# Shelley Kinder

Shelley lives in Indiana with her husband and four amazing little masterpieces who keep her on her toes. When she's not writing, Shelley likes reading, photography, family time, art projects, seventy degree days, and worship music. Shelley also enjoys semi-annual road trips to Rhode Island, where she lived for ten years, met her husband, and had kids.

*The Masterpiece* is Shelley's second children's book. She loves how her mom, Kathi Green Nixon, brought the story to life with such stunning illustrations. Shelley also wrote *Not So Scary Jerry* (Clear Fork Publishing), which Kirkus Reviews called "a charming monster tale with an appealing theme."

To learn more about Shelley and to see if you've found all the hidden paint brushes in this book, visit ShelleyKinder.com.

# Kathi Green Nixon

At the edge of Leo, Indiana, somewhere between the buffalo farm and the Amish country store lives artist Kathi Green Nixon. She wasn't always an illustrator. She spent her career as a graphic designer at a large corporation until retiring in 2017.

Now happily drawing and painting in her home studio, *The Masterpiece* came about when her daughter Shelley wrote the story, Kathi read it, and they immediately decided to collaborate on creating the book. Callie at Clear Fork Publishing agreed to the pairing, and the dream became a reality.

*The Masterpiece* is her first picture book.

CPSIA information can be obtained
at www.ICGtesting.com
Printed in the USA
LVHW070220080119
602986LV00013B/406/P